Pirates are Stealing our COWS

By Martin Remphry

Crabtree Publishing Company

www.crabtreebooks.com

Crabtree Publishing Company
www.crabtreebooks.com
1-800-387-7650

616 Welland Ave.
St. Catharines, ON
L2M 5V6

PMB 59051, 350 Fifth Ave.
59th Floor,
New York, NY 10118

Published by Crabtree Publishing Company in 2015

First published in 2013 by Franklin Watts
(A division of Hachette Children's Books)

Text and illustration © Martin Remphry 2013

Series editor: Melanie Palmer
Series advisor: Catherine Glavina
Series designer: Peter Scoulding
Editors: Jackie Hamley, Kathy Middleton
Proofreader and
   notes to adults: Shannon Welbourn
Production coordinator and
   Prepress technician: Margaret Amy Salter
Print coordinator: Katherine Berti

Printed in Hong Kong/082014/BK20140613

Pirates really did steal three Guernsey cows from the Channel Island of Brecqhou. But what did pirates want with cows?
For Zak Taylor – M.R.

Library and Archives Canada
Cataloguing in Publication

Remphry, Martin, author
   Pirates are stealing our cows / by Martin Remphry.

(Race ahead with reading)
Issued in print and electronic formats.
ISBN 978-0-7787-1330-2 (bound).--
ISBN 978-0-7787-1331-9 (pbk.).--
ISBN 978-1-4271-7778-0 (pdf).--
ISBN 978-1-4271-7766-7 (html)

   I. Title.

PZ7.R277Pi 2014   j823'.92   C2014-903685-X
                                   C2014-903686-8

Library of Congress
Cataloging-in-Publication Data

Remphry, Martin, author, illustrator.
 Pirates are stealing our cows / by Martin Remphry
; illustrated by Martin Remphry.
     pages cm. -- (Race ahead with reading)
 "First published in 2013 by Franklin Watts"--
Copyright page.
  ISBN 978-0-7787-1330-2 (reinforced library
binding) -- ISBN 978-0-7787-1331-9 (pbk.) --
ISBN 978-1-4271-7778-0 (electronic pdf) --
ISBN 978-1-4271-7766-7 (electronic html)
[1. Pirates--Fiction. 2. Cows--Fiction. 3. Humorous
stories.] I. Title.

PZ7.R28383Pi 2014
[E]--dc23
                                        2014020439

Chapter 1

"Pirates are stealing our cows!"
spluttered Farmer Marchant.

Mrs. Marchant looked up from her tea.
"What would pirates want with cows?"
she wondered.

Farmer Marchant dropped his toast and

ran down to the beach in his slippers.

But Daisy, Buttercup, and Milkshake were already sailing away from the tiny island. Their stripe-shirted captors waved their cutlasses in the air.

Mrs. Marchant poured herself a fresh cup
of tea and telephoned the police.

"I would like to report the theft of our cows
by pirates. They are called Daisy, Buttercup,
and Milkshake."

"Funny names for pirates," said the officer.
"Daisy, Buttercup, and Milkshake are our
cows!" snapped Mrs. Marchant.

"Whatever their names are, pirates don't
steal cows. They steal treasure. Anyway,
if we tried to arrest them, our police cars
would sink," the officer snapped back.

Farmer Marchant stomped into the kitchen and shook the sand from his slippers.

"I'll go after those cow-stealing sea dogs myself!" he growled, whisking the tablecloth off the table from under the teapot.

Farmer Marchant dragged the cows' water trough to the beach. He tied the tablecloth to a pitchfork like a sail. Mrs. Marchant handed him some sandwiches and pushed him off.

"Make sure you bring them back in time for milking," she called as he paddled with his shovel out to sea.

Chapter 2

The captain peered down at
the water trough bobbing
beside his battleship.

"What are you doing sailing in a water trough?" he called. "Looking for my cows," replied Farmer Marchant. "They were stolen by pirates!"

"Pirates don't steal cows. They only steal baboons," shouted the captain.

"Don't you mean doubloons?" asked the farmer.

"Pirates have treasure chests stuffed full of baboons. It says so in all the storybooks. Anyway, I'm far too busy hunting submarines to go chasing after pirates."

Farmer Marchant watched the battleship disappear over the horizon. Then...

CRUNCH! A submarine periscope rose up right through the bottom of his water trough.

Farmer Marchant peered into the metal tube.

"Has anyone down there seen any pirates with cows?" he called.

"Pirates don't have cows," said a voice from below. "They have parrots. Cows would fall off their shoulders. Anyway, we're on the lookout for battleships, not pirates."

"Well, unless I repair this hole, I'll be coming to the bottom of the sea with you. Can you drop me off on that island over there?" asked Farmer Marchant.

Chapter 3

Farmer Marchant watched the submarine

sink back under the waves.

Moooooo!

The farmer spun around. There, eating grass under a palm tree, stood Daisy, Buttercup, and Milkshake.

Behind them, three very embarrassed pirates fidgeted in front of their ship, which was now stuck in the sand.

"Well?" asked Farmer Marchant, crossing his arms. "Why did you steal my cows?" One pirate shuffled his wooden leg. "We ran out of milk, and Captain Sprat was thirsty," he mumbled.

"But we're not very good at milking."

The pirates showed their silver hook hands.

"We were so busy trying to fill the captain's

bowl that we didn't see the island ahead."

"And who is Captain Sprat?" asked Farmer Marchant.

One of the pirates handed Farmer Marchant a small black-and-white kitten.

"Captain Sprat is the ship's cat," mumbled the pirates.

Chapter 4

The pirates were truly sorry that they had stolen Daisy, Buttercup, and Milkshake, and promised to make it up to the farmer and Mrs. Marchant.

When they had dug the pirate ship out of the sand, everyone sailed back to the farm.

As soon as they landed, Mrs. Marchant put the pirates to work. She gave their grubby pirate clothes to the scarecrow and handed them pitchforks and clean overalls.

Flinty Sharp mucked out the pigsty.

Scratch'em Matchan collected the eggs.

Crusher Chesney dug the potatoes.

"Breakfast!" called Mrs. Marchant from the kitchen door, banging a large frying pan with her wooden spoon.

Chapter Five

"A farmer's breakfast is much nicer than a pirate's," munched Flinty Sharp, buttering a seventh slice of toast with his cutlass. "And you don't feel seasick while you're eating it."

"All we get on the ship are sardines and biscuits," added Crusher Chesney.

"I quite like being a farmer," said

Scratch'em Matchan. "Can you teach

me how to sail your tractor?"

"You'll have plenty of time to learn," said

Mrs. Marchant, looking out the window as

she scooped more fried eggs onto their plates.

"It looks like someone is stealing your ship!"

The pirates dropped their toast and eggs and scrambled down to the beach, just in time to see their ship being sailed away by three rather unusual pirates.

"Looks like Daisy, Buttercup, and Milkshake got a taste for the pirate life!" laughed Farmer Marchant.

Notes for Adults

These entertaining, first chapter books help children build up their reading skills so they can move on to longer books. Fun illustrations and bite-sized chapters encourage young readers to take the driver's seat and *Race Ahead with Reading*.

THE FOLLOWING BEFORE, DURING, AND AFTER READING ACTIVITY SUGGESTIONS SUPPORT LITERACY SKILL DEVELOPMENT AND CAN ENRICH SHARED READING EXPERIENCES:

BEFORE

1. Make reading fun! Choose a time to read when you and the reader are relaxed and have time to share the story together. Don't forget to give praise! Children learn best in a positive environment.

2. Before reading, ask the reader to look at the title and illustration on the cover of the book **Pirates are Stealing our Cows**. Invite them to make predictions about what will happen in the story. They may make use of prior knowledge and make connections to other stories they have heard or read about pirates or similar characters.

DURING

3. Encourage readers to determine unfamiliar words themselves by using clues from the text and illustrations.

4. During reading, encourage the child to review his or her understanding and see if they want to revise their predictions midway. Encourage the reader to make text-to-text connections, choosing a part of the story that reminds them of another story they have read; and text-to-self connections, choosing a part of the story that relates to their own personal experiences; and text-to-world connections, choosing a part of the story that reminds them of something that happened in the real world.

AFTER

5. Ask the reader who the main characters are in this story. Have the child retell the story in their own words. Ask him or her to think about the predictions they made before reading the story. How were they the same or different?

DISCUSSION QUESTIONS FOR KIDS

6. Throughout this story, Farmer Marchant and his wife have a difficult time getting help from people who believe "pirates don't steal cows." What problems does Farmer Marchant have to solve while trying to find his cows?

7. Choose one of the illustrations from the story. How do the details in the picture help you understand a part of the story better? Or, what do they tell you that is not in the text?

8. The author uses humor throughout the story. What funny or unusual things do the different characters—including the animals—do?

9. In the end, the pirates decide they like being farmers. How do you think they will manage? Create your own version of Chapter 6.

10. What moral, or lesson, can you take from this story?

11. Create your own story or drawing about a problem or challenge you had and how you solved it.